THE LEGEND OF DAVE THE VILLAGER 30

by Dave Villager

Second Print Edition (September 2020)

www.davethevillager.com
www.facebook.com/davevillager

Email me at: davevillagerauthor@gmail.com

BOOK THIRTY:
The Children of Herobrine Part 2

PROLOGUE

"General Porkins?" said Porkins. "Who's that?"

"He's the evil version of you," said Carl. "But he looks a lot cooler because he's got an eyepatch."

Carl had no idea how General Porkins was still alive, or why he was now a blue ghost, but he knew from experience that the pigman was not someone to be messed with.

"Golems, attack!" yelled Carl.

The ten iron golems dashed forward, rushing to meet the ghostly blue pigman as he ran towards them.

The first golem to reach the general tried to biff him in the face, but General Porkins blocked the blow with his iron arm. Then another golem ran forward and swung at him, but General Porkins lifted his other iron arm and blocked that blow too. Even though he looked like a ghost, he was still solid, it seemed.

"Wowza!" said Porkins. "That chap's got two iron arms!"

"I told you he was cooler than you," said Carl.

Now it was General Porkins's turn to attack. He pushed against the ground with one of his iron arms and launched himself into the air, landing on the shoulders of one of the golems. Then POW, he biffed the golem's head clean off. Then he jumped off of that golem onto the other golem and used both of his iron arms to pull its head clean off.

"Good grief!" said Porkins.

"Who are you two?" demanded the general, looking at Carl and Porkins. "Are you the blighters who destroyed my universe?"

Carl realized that although he had seen General Porkins before, General Porkins had never seen him.

"You've got the wrong guys," said Carl. "We're innocent. Can't you tell from my lovely innocent face?"

"You'll pay for this," growled General Porkins. "You will pay!"

The remaining iron golems ran towards General Porkins. The general launched himself into the air once more using his iron arms, then uppercutted another golem's head off.

"Stop this tomfoolery right now!" said Porkins, aiming his bow at his evil doppelgänger.

"Judging by your good looks, I suppose you're the other universe version of me?" said General Porkins. "Are you behind the destruction of my universe?"

"No-one is behind anything," said Carl. "Stop being an idiot! We weren't the ones who destroyed your universe, Heroprime was."

"Maybe you helped him," said General Porkins.

"Look," said Carl, "I'm sorry for what happened to your universe, but we're not the ones responsible. So stop being an idiot and calm down."

Another iron golem tried to punch General Porkins, but the general grabbed the golem's arm with both of his iron arms and yanked it out of the socket. Then *KAPOW*, he swung the arm like a club, sending the iron golem tumbling backward.

"Fire at him, Porkins!" yelled Carl

"I don't know if I should," said Porkins. "Maybe the poor chap's just scared."

"He's not a baby ocelot!" said Carl. "He's a crazy killer with two iron arms!"

"I thought iron arms were cool?" said Porkins.

"Just shoot him!" yelled Carl.

TWANG! Porkins fired an arrow at General Porkins. Porkins had always been one of the best shots that Carl had ever seen, and his aim was right on target. The arrow whizzed through the air straight towards the general. But just before the arrow hit him, General Porkins held up one of his metal arms, and the arrow bounced harmlessly off the palm of his hand.

"Oh, crumbs," said Porkins.

The arrow may have failed to take General Porkins out, but it was enough to distract him, and one of the iron golems grabbed him from behind, lifting the general into the air and pinning his metal arms to his side.

"Get off, you scoundrel!" General Porkins screamed. "You will pay! You will all pay!"

Carl was having a hard time figuring out exactly what was going on with General Porkins's body. He was blue and see-through, like a ghost, but his body seemed to be solid.

The other remaining golems gathered around the golem holding General Porkins, guarding him so he couldn't escape. The general struggled and squirmed, but he couldn't break free of the iron golem's tight grip.

"Right," said Carl, addressing the general. "Since I've got you here, and we've got some time to kill, tell me how you survived when your universe was destroyed."

"When *you* destroyed my universe, you mean?" said General Porkins.

"How many times, you bozo," said Carl, rolling his eyes, "it wasn't us, it was Heroprime."

"Listen, old bean," said Porkins, "I know what it's like to lose all your people. In our universe, I'm the only pigman left. It can get jolly lonely."

6

"So go on," Carl said to the general, "how did you survive?"

"I still don't know," said General Porkins. "I think it was because I was holding that blasted portal device shortly before the universe was destroyed. Some of its energy must have stayed on me, as when my universe was obliterated, I ended up flickering through different realities. I saw them passing in front of my eyes like some kind of nightmare. I don't know how long I spent plunging through that endless vortex of worlds, unable to escape, but somehow I managed to find my way back here, to my universe. Now I'm going to get my revenge on the blaggards responsible if it's the last thing I do."

"I hate to break it to you," said Carl, "but the blaggard responsible is dead. Heroprime destroyed your universe, and then he destroyed himself. There's no-one to have revenge on."

"Then I will take my vengeance out on you, creeper," snarled the general.

"You could do that," said Carl, "but I've got someone better you can take revenge on."

"What are you blathering about, creeper?" said General Porkins.

"Scrap what I said just now," said Carl. "Heroprime is actually alive. And I know where you can find him."

"Okay then, creeper," said General Porkins. "You have

7

my attention."

CHAPTER ONE

That Dude Can Monstermax

"That dude can monstermax?" said Slimoth, looking up at Enderbrine. "We're in big trouble."

Spidroth looked up in horror at the gigantic black tentacles pouring out of Enderbrine's mouth. Each of them was thicker than a tree trunk and they reached up, up, up towards the sky; so many of them that Spidroth and the others were cast in shadow.

"HURGH HURGH HURRRRGH!!!" screamed Enderbrine. "HRRRAAAAGGHHH!!!!!"

With a final explosion of tentacles, Enderbrine's normal body was gone, and in its place was the biggest creature that Spidroth had ever seen: a colossal mass of huge black tentacles sitting on the side of the mountain, towering over them all. Behind the tentacles, Spidroth caught a glimpse of a single pink eye above a glowing purple mouth. Enderbrine's monstermax form was nothing but tentacles, one huge pink eye that looked like an enderman's eye and a gigantic mouth: it truly was a

9

horrific sight.

"Bwark," said Cluck Lee, looking up at the gigantic monster. As good a fighter as the chicken was, it was clear that Cluck Lee knew that he didn't stand a chance against Enderbrine now.

"Let's show this fiend that he's not the only one who can monstermax," said Necroth.

"Are you sure you're going to be able to monstermax again so soon?" Vioroth asked her brother.

"I don't think I have a choice," said Necroth. "It's going to take all three of us to defeat that monster."

All three of us, thought Spidroth sadly. She hated the idea that her siblings would have to fight this battle without her, but what use would she be? They could monstermax and she couldn't: She was still trapped in the body of a chicken. Yes, she was now a chicken wearing an iron golem suit, but without being able to monstermax, she wouldn't stand a chance against Enderbrine.

"HUUUUURRRRAAAAAGGGGHH!!!!!" Enderbrine roared, smashing one of his tentacles down towards them.

"Take cover, dudes!" Slimoth yelled.

Spidroth watched as Slimoth ran forward, his eyes glowing with green light, then *KAASHOOOOOM*, he instantly transformed into a colossal green slime monster. Slimoth's monstermax form had no legs, but he did have a head and two gloopy arms, and he used one of those arms to block the black tentacle. In his monstermax form, Slimoth's face looked just like a slime, and his body was gloopy and could change shape.

Enderbrine smashed another huge tentacle down towards them, and Slimoth blocked that with his other arm, but he was really struggling. Enderbrine's monstermax form was about four times the size of Slimoth's.

"DUDES, I COULD REALLY DO WITH SOME HELP!" Slimoth shouted.

"I'm coming brother!" shouted Vioroth. Her eyes began glowing purple, her skin crackled with electricity and then *FAAASHOOOOOM*, she transformed into a colossal three-headed wolf with gray fur: her monstermax form.

Necroth put his hand on Spidroth's golem shoulder.

"Spidroth, get everyone out of here," he said. "This is going to get messy."

Necroth ran forward, his eyes glowing white and his body crackling with white electricity.

"GYAAAAAGGGHHH!!!!" he screamed, as four gigantic white wings burst out of his back. He flew up into the sky as he transformed, and soon he had changed into his monstermax form: a gigantic white four-winged phantom.

"Wow," said Steve, looking up at Vioroth, Slimoth,

Necroth and Enderbrine in their monstermax forms. "I want to turn into a huge monster as well!"

"Well, you can't," said Spidroth. "Now come on, let's get out of here."

Spidroth ushered Steve, Jean-Cowphio, Sensei Coach, Cluck Lee, and all the chickens down the slope of the mountain.

THOOOOOM!!!!

Spidroth looked back and saw that the battle had begun. Slimoth was punching Enderbrine with his huge slime arms, Vioroth's three wolf heads were biting Enderbrine's tentacles, and Necroth was weaving through the tentacles as he flew, biting one of them after the other.

Spidroth felt so useless. She should be with them, she knew, but she was trapped in her useless chicken body.

The mountain shook as Herobrine's children fought. Enderbrine's colossal tentacles were smashing against the slopes of the mountain, sending stone blocks flying everywhere.

"Should we help them?" Steve asked Spidroth.

"There's nothing we can do against that beast," said Spidroth. "This is up to my brothers and my sister now."

Once they'd got a safe distance away, Spidroth and the others turned to watch the battle. Her siblings were doing their best against Enderbrine, but Enderbrine was so huge and had so many tentacles, that it was a tough battle. For every tentacle that Vioroth or Necroth bit off, or Slimoth broke with his massive gloopy arms, Enderbrine grew two more.

"Do you think they can defeat him?" Sensei Coach asked.

"I don't know," said Spidroth.

Then, just as it looked like Spidroth's siblings might be able to hold their own, the battle started to go wrong. Enderbrine managed to grab Necroth with one of his black tentacles, the tentacle wrapping tightly around him so that he couldn't fly. Another tentacle wrapped itself around Vioroth's body, lifting her into the air as her wolf heads snapped and barked. More tentacles tried to wrap around Slimoth, and he had to turn himself into liquid to get out of their grip. A torrent of green liquid came rushing down the mountain's slope, straight towards Spidroth and the others.

"Uh-oh," said Jean-Cowphio, "this does not look good".

There was so much green liquid rushing towards them, that Spidroth knew that they had no chance to escape in time. The liquid would hit them and wash them down the mountain, probably to their deaths.

In that moment, Spidroth knew what she had to do.

Come on, she told herself, *it's up to you now.*

For the past few days, ever since she had turned back

into a chicken, Spidroth had been trying to transform back into her old body. But this time was different: she wasn't trying to transform back into her original body, she was trying to monstermax.

Spidroth concentrated and concentrated, the sweat dripping down her white feathers. The green liquid was almost upon them now, but she tried to blank it out, closing her eyes and only thinking about monstermaxing.

"Come on," she yelled, "come on, come on, come on!"

Spidroth knew that her body was nothing but the ordinary body of a chicken, but that same body had monstermaxed before, back when she'd fought the red creeper queen and during the rebellion against the Empress. The machine at Laboratory 303 had only transformed what her chicken body had looked like, it hadn't actually given her her original body back. Her original body was now nothing but an empty husk trapped in the void below the bedrock.

"Come on, you useless chicken," Spidroth told herself. "You can do this!"

Spidroth's eyes were closed, but she could hear the green liquid getting closer and closer towards them, rushing down the mountainside. Cluck Lee and the amber chickens were squawking in panic, but Spidroth just drowned them out and concentrated on the task at hand.

She could feel a slight crackle of electricity inside her feathers, and it was growing stronger by the second.

"Come on, fool!" she shouted. "Come on, come on, come on—"

Then, suddenly, Spidroth's entire chicken body exploded with electricity. Her eyes glowed red and the iron golem suit she was wearing exploded in a burst of red light.

"YAAAAAAAAAAAAAAAAAGGGHHH!!!!!!!" Spidroth screamed.

"Spidroth!" Sensei Coach yelled. "What's happening to you?"

"Bring... everyone... further down the mountain!" Spidroth gasped. "Get out of here!"

"What about you?" asked Steve.

"Just go!" Spidroth yelled.

Steve and Sensei Coach did as they were asked, rushing down the mountain with Jean-Cowphio and the chickens.

GATHOOOOOOOOOOOOOOOOOOSSSH!!!!!!

in an explosion of red light, Spidroth transformed into a gigantic red chicken—her monstermax form. She placed both of her huge wings down on the ground to form a wall, and the green liquid splashed against it, stopping in its tracks. Slimoth's slime face appeared in the middle of liquid.

"THANKS, SIS," he said. "HEY! YOU'VE

MONSTERMAXED!"

"I HAVE," said Spidroth.

"UM, I DON'T REMEMBER YOUR MONSTERMAX FORM BEING SO CHICKENEY," said Slimoth.

Spidroth looked up the mountain. Enderbrine was pulling Vioroth and Necroth towards his huge glowing purple mouth with his tentacles, preparing to eat them.

"COME ON!" Spidroth yelled at Slimoth. "WE HAVE TO GET UP THERE AND SAVE THEM!"

Spidroth ran up the slope with her huge chicken legs, the ground shaking with every step. Slimoth slurped up the slope behind her in his liquid form.

As Spidroth approached him, Enderbrine tried to grab her with his gigantic tentacles. Spidroth had to duck, weave and jump to avoid getting caught, until finally she reached the tentacles that were holding Vioroth and Necroth. Spidroth grabbed the tentacle holding Vioroth with her beak, biting down on it and tearing it off. At the same time, Slimoth rose up from his liquid state and punched the tentacle that was holding Necroth.

Necroth and Vioroth landed on the ground at the same time. Spidroth and Slimoth ran over to join them and the four siblings were reunited once more, the four of them facing down Enderbrine together.

"I like your new monstermax form, sister," said Necroth, as he beat his wings and rose into the air.

Spidroth was surprised to hear that her brother could use his normal voice when in monstermax form.

"YEAH, I GUESS CHICKENS ARE PRETTY COOL," said Slimoth.

Even though they were facing a gigantic monster, Spidroth was pleased to be fighting alongside all three of her siblings once more. It had been over a thousand years since the four of them had gone into battle together.

Even if we lose today, thought Spidroth, *this will be a battle that the bards will sing of until the end of time.*

"HUUUUURRRRUURK!!!!!!!!!!!!!" Enderbrine roared, sending his tentacles flying towards them.

Spidroth, Vioroth, Slimoth and Necroth rushed forward to meet him, and a furious battle began.

*

Isabella watched in horror as the five children of Herobrine battled on the mountain. All of them were so gigantic that the battle shook the earth itself, each punch and each blow echoing across the mountain range.

They're going to destroy us all, Isabella thought.

Ever since Herobrine had escaped from his glass prison in New Diamond City, Isabella, like many of the other witches, had started losing faith in him. After his escape, Herobrine's first command had been to free his firstborn son, Enderbrine. Isabella had heard the stories of what had happened the last time Enderbrine was free: how he had wiped out entire cities while in his monstermax form, and how Herobrine had only just managed to subdue his son and imprison him in an ender chest. If the tales were to be believed, Herobrine had almost been slain in the battle.

In the past, Isabella had always known Herobrine to be clever and calculating, sometimes spending years formulating his plans, but since he had escaped from New Diamond City, he had been more reckless and impatient. When Dave the villager and his friends had defeated Herobrine amongst the ruins of the old Diamond City, something had snapped in his mind. Whether it was the humiliation of defeat or something else, Isabella didn't know, but she knew that Herobrine was no longer the man that she, and generations of her family before her, had followed for all these years.

Isabella ran up the mountain towards the battle, holding on tight to the silver trident in her hand. The Trident of Hexaros had been in her family for generations, passed down from mother to daughter. Long ago, before they had dedicated themselves to Herobrine, Isabella's family had been part of a clan of powerful witches. When Isabella's great great great grandmother had left the clan, she had taken the trident with her. Isabella didn't know how old the Trident was, but, if the stories were to be believed, it dated back all the way to the time of the Old People, who had often mixed science and magic together to create extremely powerful weapons. The Trident of Hexaros had one purpose: to suck out the magic from powerful beings.

The mountain was shaking from the battle, but Isabella kept going. Several times she stumbled and fell to the ground, but she kept picking herself back up and continuing the climb.

Time to end this once and for all, she thought to herself. *It's time to put an end to Herobrine's children.*

CHAPTER TWO

Surprise Guests

"Oh no," gasped Herobrine, looking up at the gigantic black tentacles rising above them.

Dave was amazed to see that Herobrine, for once, looked scared.

This monster must be pretty bad if Herobrine's scared of it, Dave thought.

Dave had no idea what the gigantic black-tentacled creature was, but it was the distraction that he needed. He took the Dimensional Portal Device out of his pocket and pressed the button. The blue portal fizzed into life in front of him. Herobrine was so busy looking at the giant tentacle creature that he didn't even notice the portal.

For a moment, nothing happened.

Where are Carl and Porkins? Dave wondered.

Then, finally, someone jumped out of the portal. But it wasn't Porkins or Carl; instead, it was a see-through blue figure. The figure flickered for a moment, and then its see-through blue body became solid and pink, and Dave realized who it was.

"General Porkins!" gasped Dave.

Dave was very confused. The last time he'd seen the evil version of Porkins, the pigman had dissolved away with the rest of the Mirror Universe, but here he was, alive and well. Then Carl and the real Porkins jumped out of the portal behind him, accompanied by six iron golems. Where the rest of the iron golems were, Dave had no idea. He had left Carl and Porkins with ten.

"Er, what's going on?" Dave asked Carl, looking at General Porkins.

"Long story," said Carl.

Finally, Herobrine turned his eyes away from the enormous black tentacles and noticed Carl, Porkins, General Porkins and the golems.

"You!" said General Porkins, pointing at Herobrine."You scoundrel! You cad! You will pay for what you've done!"

Dave gave Carl a confused look.

"He thinks that Herobrine is Heroprime," Carl whispered.

"Why does he think that?" asked Dave.

"Because I told him," said Carl.

Before Herobrine could realize what was going on, General Porkins ran towards him.

"Golems, attack!" yelled Carl.

The six iron golems all charged towards Herobrine as well, and Porkins began firing arrows at him.

Herobrine easily dodged the arrows and began fighting the iron golems.

Dave's mum and dad ran over to him, and Dave's mum pulled him in for a hug.

"Oh Dave," she said. "We were so worried about you!"

"Thanks, Mum," said Dave. "But you and Dad need to get somewhere safe. Carl, grab my parents and get as far away from here as you can."

"What about you, son?" asked Dave's dad.

"I'm going to deal with Herobrine," said Dave, reaching into his bag and pulling out the Shadow Blade.

"Come on, Mr and Mrs Dave," said Carl, picking up Dave's parents in his netherite golem arms.

"Wait!" shouted Dave's mum. "Dave, come with us!"

"Get out of here now!" Dave said to Carl.

Carl nodded, then began running down the mountain, holding Dave's parents.

"Daaaaaave!" Dave's mum shouted. "Be careful!"

Dave turned towards Herobrine. Herobrine had now destroyed all of the iron golems and was walking towards General Porkins.

"Time to die!" shouted General Porkins, tensing his two iron arms. The pigman ran towards Herobrine, ready to strike him down. Herobrine lazily stepped to one side to avoid the general's punch, then *POW*, he punched the pigman and sent him flying. The general went hurtling through the air, before hitting the ground and rolling down the mountain.

Porkins (the normal one) fired another barrage of arrows at Herobrine, but the arrows just shattered as they hit him, their broken shafts falling uselessly to the ground.

All of Herobrine's attention was focused on Porkins, and Dave knew that this might be his only chance. As Porkins notched his bow to fire another arrow, Dave ran around the side of Herobrine, holding the Shadow Blade.

Here goes, thought Dave. He ran towards Herobrine, ready to strike him down.

KRAKOOOOOOM!!!!!

Suddenly the whole mountain began to shake. Dave fell, dropping the Shadow Blade in the snow.

WATHOOOOM!!!! DAKOOOOOM!!!!!!

On the lower slopes of the mountain, an epic battle was taking place, Dave saw. The gigantic black tentacle monster was now fighting off four other gigantic creatures, one of which, Dave was surprised to see, was Spidroth's monstermax chicken form. Dave had no idea why Spidroth was on the mountain, or how she'd been able to monstermax again, but he had other things to worry about right now. He picked up the Shadow Blade and got back to his feet.

Porkins had managed to stay on his feet, and he fired another arrow at Herobrine. Herobrine grabbed the arrow in midair, then ran forward towards Porkins, moving at an incredible speed.

He's going to kill Porkins! thought Dave. Dave ran towards Herobrine as fast as he could, clutching the Shadow Blade in his hand.

Then a gigantic black tentacle smashed into the side of the mountain and Dave fell over once more. Herobrine and Porkins fell over as well.

The battle on the slopes below was destroying the mountain, Dave saw. Spidroth and the other monsters were just too big, and every time they hit each other, the entire mountain shook.

Dave tried to push himself to his feet again, but before he could, a gigantic white flying creature, that looked like a phantom with four wings, went hurtling into the mountain slope below him.

KADOOOOOM!!!!!!

Suddenly the entire top of the mountain collapsed, and Dave found himself tumbling down the mountainside, amongst a landslide of stone blocks and snow.

CHAPTER THREE

Sibling Fight

Spidroth hated to admit it, but it was good to be back in her monstermax form once more. But it was even better to be fighting alongside Vioroth, Slimoth, and Necroth again.

Spidroth and her siblings were putting up a good fight against Enderbrine, but the black tentacle monster was just too big, and for every tentacle they destroyed, Enderbrine seemed to grow two more.

Another giant tentacle crashed down towards her, and Spidroth caught it in her beak. She crunched down on the tentacle, then ripped it off—*SHROWK!!* But then another tentacle smashed into her from the side, sending her rolling down the mountain.

To her left, Spidroth saw Vioroth fighting off more tentacles, leaping on them and biting the tentacles off with her three wolf heads. Slimoth was using his two big green arms to punch the tentacles, and Necroth was sweeping through the air, attacking the tentacles with his four wings.

Their battle was taking its toll on the mountain, with

each punch and each attack shaking the mountain to its core.

Destroying the tentacles isn't working, thought Spidroth, *we need to attack the eye.*

Behind the mass of black tentacles, Spidroth could see Enderbrine's gaping purple mouth. There was a bright purple glow coming from inside his throat, and above the mouth was a huge pink eye.

Spidroth charged towards Enderbrine's eye, ducking and jumping out of the way of the tentacles that flew towards her. She was almost there, when a tentacle managed to wrap around her, pinning her to the ground. Spidroth struggled, using her gigantic chicken feet to push herself forward, but Enderbrine was too strong. He lifted her into the air with his tentacle and held her above his gigantic purple mouth.

He's going to eat me! thought Spidroth in horror.

Enderbrine let go of her, and she began falling down towards his mouth, but at the last minute, she flapped her wings. Her wings weren't powerful enough to let her fly properly, but she managed to flutter forward, over the mouth, and land on Enderbrine's gigantic pink eye, feet first.

"AIIIIIIIIIIIIEEEEEEEEE!!!!!!!!!!" Enderbrine screamed, as Spidroth's feet plunged into his eyeball.

A huge black tentacle slapped into Spidroth, sending

her flying. She landed hard on the mountain slope, but her mission had been a success: Enderbrine was flailing and screaming; his single eye closed in pain.

"YO, I THINK YOU HURT HIM, SIS," said Slimoth.

"WE NEED TO ATTACK THE EYE!" Spidroth told her siblings. "THAT'S HIS WEAK POINT!"

Enderbrine was still squirming around in pain, flailing his tentacles. Spidroth knew that now was their chance: Enderbrine was distracted; this might be the only opportunity they had to defeat him. She, Vioroth and Slimoth rushed towards the center of Enderbrine's tentacles, heading towards his eye. Necroth flew above them, weaving past the flailing tentacles.

This is it, thought Spidroth, *this is our chance to take him down.*

Then Spidroth felt something small prick her right foot. For a moment, she thought she'd just trodden on a sharp bit of stone, but then she began to feel funny. Her legs felt weak, and she tripped over, skidding across the ground.

What's happening to me? she wondered. *What's going on?*

*

Isabella pulled the trident out of the giant red chicken's

leg. The chicken tumbled over, smashing onto the ground with a force that made the mountain shake.

The trident was glowing with red light now, a light that was so bright that Isabella had to squint.

"It worked!" Isabella grinned. The trident had sucked all the energy out of the giant chicken. Isabella aimed the trident up, then *FZZAM*, she fired the red energy into the sky, disposing of it for good.

One down, Isabella thought. *Four to go.*

The giant white phantom, the three-headed wolf and the green slime monster had come back to check on the giant chicken.

Good, thought Isabella, *gather together. That will make my job all the easier.*

The giant white phantom landed next to the chicken.

"Are you all right, Spidroth?" The phantom asked.

So, that giant chicken is Spidrothbrine, thought Isabella. She'd always heard that Spidrothbrine's monstermax form was a big ball of spider legs and red eyes, but she supposed that must have changed. She knew who the other creatures were: the white phantom was Necrothbrine, the three-headed wolf was Viorothbrine, and the green slime monster was Slimothbrine. Isabella knew that Enderbrine was the most dangerous of Herobrine's children, but he was currently flailing about in pain from when the giant chicken had landed in his eye, so she was going to take him out last.

Isabella ran up behind Slimothbrine, the giant green slime monster, and plunged the trident into his back. At first, Slimothbrine didn't even seem to feel it, but then he began jerking about and choking.

"AK!" he gasped, his voice booming across the mountain. "WHAT'S... HAPPENING TO ME?!"

Isabella pulled the trident out of Slimothbrine. The trident was glowing green now, and she aimed it at the sky and fired. The green energy went hurtling up into the air, never to be used again.

Slimothbrine and Spidrothbrine were both convulsing on the ground, with Viorothbrine and Necrothbrine looking on in confusion. Isabella was so small compared to them that they didn't even notice her. She quickly ran over towards the giant white phantom then plunged the trident into one of its wings. Before Necrothbrine could react, she pulled the trident out and blasted the white energy she'd sucked up into the sky.

This is too easy, thought Isabella, grinning to herself. Soon the world would be safe from Herobrine's monstrous children once more.

As Necrothbrine began shaking and convulsing, Isabella ran around the side of him, towards Viorothbrine: the giant three-headed wolf. She had almost reached the wolf's legs when one of its heads spotted her.

"I SEE YOU!" roared the wolf. "WHAT HAVE YOU DONE?!"

The colossal wolf lunged towards Isabella, trying to grab her in its massive jaws. Isabella quickly threw the Trident like a javelin. The Trident flew through the air and struck the wolf in one of its noses.

"GAAAAAH!" Viorothbrine screamed as she tripped over and tumbled forward, coming to a stop right in front of Isabella. Isabella quickly climbed up the snout of the wolf with the trident in its nose and pulled it out. The trident was glowing with purple energy.

"WHAT... IS... THAT?" gasped the wolf, looking at the trident.

"This is everything that made you special," said Isabella. "This is all your power; all the power that your father gave you."

Isabella pointed the trident at the sky.

"And now," said Isabella, "it's going to be gone for good."

FSSSHAM!!! Isabella fired the purple energy up into the air, where it disappeared into the blue sky.

Isabella jumped off of the wolf's snout, landing on the ground. The giant grey wolf, the giant white phantom, the giant green slime monster, and the giant red chicken were all lying on the ground, their bodies shaking.

"I've taken your power!" Isabella told them. "In a few

minutes, you'll all be normal. You'll all be powerless."

Now, thought Isabella, *it's time for Enderbrine.*

Suddenly a black tentacle wrapped itself around her, taking her by surprise.

"No!" Isabella yelled. She tried to use the trident, but her arms were pinned to her sides by the tentacle. The tentacle threw her towards Enderbrine's huge purple mouth.

"Waaaaaaaaaa!" screamed Isabella, as she went flying towards the giant mouth. She tried to keep hold of the trident, but she was flying through the air too fast and lost her grip. The Trident fell from her hands, and she went hurtling into the gaping purple mouth.

*

Spidroth tried to get to her feet, but she felt too weak.

She looked around and saw that her siblings were in the same position as she was, still in their monstermax forms, but all of them weakened and lying on the ground. Spidroth had no idea who the witch with the trident was, but she had stolen their power. Spidroth could feel herself getting weaker by the second.

"Arrrrgh!" Spidroth screamed. She could feel her bones changing shape and her body shrinking.

Please, she thought, *don't let me turn back into a*

chicken again!

Finally, her body stopped transforming. To Spidroth's relief, when she looked down she saw red hands rather than white wings.

I'm back in my old body, she thought, feeling relieved. *That's something, at least.*

She looked over and saw that her siblings were back in their normal bodies as well.

"Dude," said Slimoth, "she took away my powers! I can't monstermax and I can't summon any slimes either."

"Oh, stop complaining, fool," said Spidroth. "I spent 1,000 years under bedrock, and until a few minutes ago I was a chicken. Things could be worse."

"Um, I think things have got worse," said Vioroth, looking up at something. "A lot worse."

Spidroth followed Vioroth's gaze and saw what her sister was looking at: Enderbrine was leering down at them with his giant pink eye, his tentacles raised and ready to smash them to pieces.

"HURR, HURR, HUUUUURR!!!" Enderbrine bellowed.

Spidroth and her siblings had fought a good fight, but there was no escape.

"It has been an honor to fight alongside you all one last time," said Necroth.

I just wish I'd got the chance to tell Dave how I feel,

thought Spidroth sadly. She hoped that wherever Dave was, he was safe.

Enderbrine shot out all his black tentacles towards them. Spidroth closed her eyes and braced herself for the end.

But the end didn't come...

KRAAAAAKOOOOOOOOOMMMMM!!!!!!!!!!!!!!!!!!!!!!!!!!!

Suddenly the entire mountain began to shake. The part of the mountain above them began to rise up and take shape, the stone transforming into a colossal figure with two arms, two legs and a head. And on the head were two glowing white eyes.

"It's dad!" gasped Slimoth.

Her brother was right, Spidroth realized. Herobrine had taken control of the top half of the mountain.

The gigantic stone Herobrine reached down and grabbed Enderbrine's tentacles, and a ferocious battle began.

"We need to get off this mountain!" yelled Spidroth.

"Yeah, I agree with you there, sis," said Slimoth.

As the humongous stone Herobrine and the gigantic black tentacle monster began to do battle, Spidroth, Slimoth, Vioroth and Necroth all began running down the mountain as fast as they could.

CHAPTER FOUR

Just Like the Good Old Days

The landslide came to a stop, and Dave found himself lying on the ground, covered in tiny stone blocks.

"Come on, old chap," said a voice. "Let's get you up."

Dave felt a cold metal hand grab his arm and looked up to see Porkins. The pigman pulled him to his feet.

They were halfway down the mountain, on a wide, flat stone plane, with a few trees scattered around. They had gone so far down that there was no longer any snow.

Carl was there as well, as were Dave's parents. Thankfully they were all okay.

Dave's mum ran over and hugged him.

"Oh, Dave!" she sobbed. "I'm so glad you're okay!"

Dave's dad came over and put a hand on his son's shoulder.

"It's good to see you, son," said Dave's dad.

"I'm just glad you're both safe," said Dave, smiling at his parents.

"Er, I hate to break up this happy reunion," said Carl,

"but I think we need to keep moving. Look up there!"

Dave looked up. The top half of the mountain had now completely collapsed, and in its place stood a colossal stone man with two glowing white eyes.

"Herobrine!" Dave gasped.

The giant stone Herobrine was fighting the gigantic black tentacle monster. From down here, Dave could see the tentacle monster more clearly; in the middle of all its black tentacles was a round body with one colossal pink eye and a gaping circular mouth that glowed with purple light. It was the strangest creature that Dave had ever seen —and he had seen a lot of strange creatures.

DOOM! The tentacle monster slapped the stone Herobrine across the face with one of its giant tentacles.

WHAM! The giant stone Herobrine retaliated by punching the tentacles out of the way.

The two colossal creatures continued to do battle, each of their punches and blows shaking the mountain.

"I think Carl is right, dear boy," said Porkins. "Very soon, there won't be any mountain left."

"What happened to General Porkins?" Dave asked.

"Who cares?" said Carl. "Hopefully he fell to his doom or something. I'm sure I don't need to remind you, but he was a pretty evil guy."

"Okay," said Dave, "let's get off the mountain."

But then, just as they were about to flee further down

the mountain, a group of ten-or-so golems ran over and surrounded them. They weren't like any golems that Dave had ever seen: they were made of some strange dark-grey substance that looked like shadow. The only part of them that wasn't dark grey was their glowing red eyes.

"Oh, great," sighed Carl. "This is all we need."

"Mum, Dad, stay behind us, said Dave.

Dave, Carl and Porkins stood in a circle, surrounding Dave's parents. Dave pulled out the Shadow Blade, Porkins pulled out his bow, and Carl flexed his big netherite arms, preparing for battle.

"Let us pass, you brutes!" Porkins said to the golems. "Or we will be forced to give you the thrashing of a lifetime!"

The golems said nothing and just charged towards them.

"Attack!" yelled Dave.

Dave ran forward to meet the shadow golems. One of the golems swung at him with its arm, but Dave parried the blow with the Shadow Blade. The sword was so sharp that it sliced the golem's arm in two. The golem tried to grab Dave with its other arm, but Dave ducked out of the way, and then thrust the Shadow Blade up, slicing off that arm as well. Without its arms, the golem lost its balance and fell face-first onto the ground. Two more golems rushed towards Dave, and he ran towards them, swinging the Shadow Blade.

To his right, Dave could see Carl doing battle with the golems in his netherite suit. The shadow golems were strong, and Carl was having to put up a good fight to defeat them.

Behind him, Dave could hear the twanging of a bow as Porkins fired arrow after arrow at the golems.

"Chaps, this is just like the good old days!" said Porkins. "Us three lads all fighting together—Dave, Carl and Porkins!"

"Yeah," said Carl, as he biffed another golem in the face, "just like old times—a load of bad guys trying to kill us. Forgive me if I don't get too sentimental."

The mountain shook once more. Dave looked up and saw the battle between the giant stone Herobrine and the massive black tentacle monster was getting more vicious. Before long, the whole mountain would collapse.

"We need to finish this battle quickly," shouted Dave, as he blocked another punch from a shadow golem. "I'm not sure how much longer this mountain is going to be standing."

Suddenly Dave heard the stomping of footsteps and, to his horror, saw more shadow golems rushing down the slope towards them.

"Oh great," said Carl, "there's more of these guys?"

The shadow golems surrounded them. There were at

least fifty of them, by Dave's count.

"I think this is going to be a tad tricky, chaps," said Porkins.

"If by tricky you mean we're going to get torn to pieces, then I agree with you," said Carl.

Dave held the Shadow Blade out in front of him, ready to do battle. The golems began to charge towards them, their heavy footsteps echoing across the stone.

There's no way we can defeat all of them, thought Dave. There were just too many.

"Ninja Squad!" Dave heard a familiar voice yell. "Kick their butts!"

Suddenly a load of ninjas appeared from out of nowhere, running up behind the shadow golems and attacking. Most of the ninjas had diamond swords, but one of them had diamond axes, Dave saw, and two of them had bows.

The ninja who had spoken wore a black outfit, but her pale face and long orange hair were exposed.

"Is that Alex?" said Carl. "What's she doing with the Ninja Squad? And what are the Ninja Squad doing here? Did one of those shadow golems knock me unconscious? Is this all some weird dream?"

"Hi Dave, hi Carl, hi Porkins!" said Alex, running over them. "It's so awesome to see you!"

"Alex, what are you doing here?" Dave asked

"There'll be time for explanations later," said Alex. "At the moment, we've got some butt to kick."

"It's good to see you again, Sensei Carl," said Avyukth-San, rushing over to see him.

"Look, Sensei Carl," said Ash, picking up an ocelot and showing it to Carl. "I've got a new cat!"

"ARRGH!" said Carl. "Get that thing away from me!"

"Sorry, Sensei," said Ash, looking upset. "When I lost my Elemental Block powers, I couldn't summon my yellow electric cat anymore, so I trained this ocelot to take its place."

"All right, chaps, that's enough catching up for now," said Porkins, "we need to defeat these golem fiends!"

A golem lumbered towards Dave, bringing its arm back and getting ready to punch him. Dave gripped the Shadow Blade tightly, ready to fight, but then something small, amber and green flew through the air in front of him and kicked the golem's head clean off.

The small amber and green thing landed in front of Dave.

"Bwark!"

"Cluck Lee!" said Dave happily.

Suddenly, an army of amber chickens rushed onto the battlefield, attacking the golems.

A cowman in a green tracksuit ran over to Dave.

"Sensei Coach," said Dave, "are these your chickens?"

"Yes they are, Dave-San," said Sensei Coach.

Then, to Dave's surprise, more familiar faces ran onto the battlefield. Steve appeared, attacking golems with an iron sword, and then Jean-Cowphio followed behind him, wearing all gold armor and holding a golden sword.

Dave ran over to Steve.

"Steve," said Dave, "why are you here? I thought you and Spidroth were going to stay back at the castle."

"Well, it all got a bit complicated, said Steve. "First there were skeletons, then I died a whole bunch of times, then there were chickens, then Spidroth got a big iron suit, then we went up a mountain, then we fought some crazy guy with tentacles coming out of his mouth, then the crazy tentacle guy turned into a giant crazy tentacle guy, then Spidroth turned into a big red chicken. You know how it is."

"Is Spidroth okay?" Dave asked.

"I'm not sure," said Steve. "I lost track of her after she turned into a giant chicken. Have we met before, by the way? You look familiar."

Dave looked up at the top of the mountain. Herobrine and the colossal tentacle creature were still doing battle, but there was no sign of Spidroth in her giant chicken form or any of the other monsters that had been fighting up there earlier.

At that moment, Dave made a decision.

"Carl," said Dave, "once all these golems are defeated, I need you to get everyone off the mountain. And I mean *completely* off the mountain. There'll be nothing left of it soon."

"Where are you going," asked Carl.

"I think Spidroth is somewhere up the mountain," said Dave. "I need to go and find her."

"Yo, man, I'm coming too," said Jean-Cowphio, running over. "Vee and her brothers were with Spidroth."

"Her brothers?" said Dave. "Those other two monsters were Spidroth's brothers?"

"Yeah," said Jean-Cowphio. "Slimoth and Necroth. They're both pretty cool guys. That big tentacle monster is their brother too, I think. Although he's not very cool. I think that weird villager guy said his name was Enderbrine."

Dave had no time to get his head around all the complicated relationships in Herobrine's family. All he wanted to do was go and make sure that Spidroth was okay.

"Come on," he said to Jean-Cowphio, "let's get moving."

CHAPTER FIVE

The Rescue

"Watch out!" shouted Jean-Cowphio as another landslide of stone blocks rushed down the slope towards them.

Dave and Jean-Cowphio jumped out of the way just in time. The mountain was falling apart all around them, with landslides and falling blocks coming from above them, and holes opening up in the mountain below them. They had to watch their step, as there were cracks in the mountain where you could see pools of lava below, and the further up they got, the worse things became.

"So tell me about this monstermax thing again, D-Dogg," said Jean-Cowphio. "Vee never really talked about that kind of thing. You know, about her weird past, and her dad, and all that stuff."

"As far as I understand it," said Dave, "all of Herobrine's kids can turn into giant monsters, but it takes a lot of energy, and they can get exhausted afterward. Spidroth, Vioroth and their brothers might be lying exhausted on the mountain, too tired to get down."

42

"Well, at least they've got their heroic boyfriends coming to save them," said Jean-Cowphio

Dave's cheeks glowed red.

"I'm not Spidroth's boyfriend," he said.

"Oh, sorry, man, my bad," said Jean-Cowphio. "I thought you dudes were together."

"Anyway," said Dave, "Vioroth isn't your girlfriend; she's your wife."

"Oh yeah," said Jean-Cowphio. "I always forget that."

They were getting closer to the epic battle on the upper slopes of the mountain now. The giant stone Herobrine and Enderbrine, Herobrine's monstrous son, were still fighting. The battle seemed to be pretty evenly matched. Every time Herobrine ripped off one of Enderbrine's colossal tentacles, Enderbrine re-grew a new one, and every time Enderbrine smashed away part of Herobrine's giant stone body, Herobrine would reach down suck up more stone from the mountain to fix himself. The only thing that was really taking damage was the mountain itself.

Dave had given up on his plan to assassinate Herobrine. He knew now that it was pointless: Herobrine was so powerful that there was no way Dave would even be able to get near enough to strike him down with the Shadow Blade. All Dave wanted to do now was get Spidroth and her siblings safely off the mountain, and then

43

get Spidroth, his parents, and all his friends as far away from here as possible. There was no way they could defeat Herobrine, so they would have to make do with escaping from him instead.

As they climbed further up, Dave and Jean-Cowphio had to avoid the rivers of lava that were flowing down the slope of the mountain. The cracks in the ground had caused some underground lava lakes to overflow their banks.

"Yo, look!" said Jean-Cowphio, pointing. "There they are!"

Dave looked up the slope and saw what Jean-Cowphio was pointing at. In the middle of a wide river of flowing lava was a tiny island, and on the island were four figures: a man with green skin, a man with dark-blue skin, Vioroth, Jean-Cowphio's wife, and Spidroth. Dave was surprised to see that Spidroth was no longer a chicken: she was back in her old body, with her red skin and her black hair, and not a feather in sight.

All four of the siblings were lying on the ground, and looked exhausted.

"All that monstermaxing must have worn them out," said Jean-Cowphio. "Vee and her brothers only monstermaxed a short while ago, so I guess they did it again too soon."

Dave and Jean-Cowphio ran up the slope towards the

lava river, getting as close to it as they dared.

"Don't worry, Vee!" yelled Jean-Cowphio. "I'm here to save you, baby!"

Vioroth, Spidroth and their brothers all looked over at Dave and Jean-Cowphio. The siblings all looked exhausted and could barely keep their eyes open.

"Dave..." gasped Spidroth. "You came to rescue me..."

Then she fainted.

"Spidroth!" Dave shouted. He reached into his bag, pulled out some sand blocks, and then placed them down —*thunk, thunk, thunk*—blocking the lava flow and building a bridge across to the island.

Dave ran straight over to Spidroth and kneeled next to her. She was out cold, so he lifted her over his shoulder.

"Come on, babycakes," said Jean-Cowphio, taking Vioroth by the hand and pulling her to her feet.

"It's good to see you, my love," said Vioroth, smiling weakly. "I thought we were done for."

Jean-Cowphio helped Spidroth's brothers to their feet as well. They were all a bit worse for wear, but apart from Spidroth, they were all conscious.

"I'm not surprised my sister has run out of energy," said the brother with the dark-blue skin, looking at Spidroth. "In the space of a few minutes, she's gone from being a chicken to monstermaxing to returning to her normal form. That has got to take it out of you."

45

"Dudes, watch out!" yelled the green-skinned brother, pointing towards the top of the mountain.

Dave looked up and saw that the giant stone Herobrine had taken a powerful hit from the black tentacle creature and was tumbling down the mountain towards them. If they didn't get out of the way in a few seconds, they would all be flattened.

"Do any of you have the energy to monstermax and get us out of here?" Dave asked.

"We can't monstermax anymore," said Vioroth, "our powers were taken from us. We can't summon mobs, we can't monstermax, we can't do anything."

Dave had to think fast. The giant stone Herobrine was so colossal that there was no way they could get out of the way in time, so there was only one solution. He placed Spidroth gently down on the ground and pulled a diamond pickaxe out of his bag.

"Follow me, and bring Spidroth," said Dave, as he began to dig straight down.

"Yo, that looks a bit cramped in there," said Jean-Cowphio, peering down into the narrow pit.

"Just get down here!" yelled Dave.

Jean-Cowphio lowered Spidroth down into the hole, passing her to Dave, and then he and the others climbed down into the hole as well. The hole was only one block wide and four blocks deep, but somehow they all managed to cram in.

DOOM, DOOM, DOOM!

They felt the mountain shake as the gigantic stone Herobrine tumbled down the slope. For a second, the small square of light above them went black as Herobrine passed overhead, and then they could see the sky again. They waited for a moment, and then heard the sound of the stone Herobrine getting back to its feet and running up the mountain once more, and then the battle between the stone Herobrine and the giant tentacle monster resumed.

"What... What's going on?" asked Spidroth, opening her eyes.

"We hid down here to avoid getting squashed by dad," said Vioroth.

"Oh... Right," said Spidroth

Dave got his pickaxe out and began digging diagonally upwards until they reached the surface. The battle between the giant stone Herobrine and Enderbrine was still raging above them.

"Come on," said Dave, "let's get out of here."

CHAPTER SIX

The Faithful Servant

Wretch looked on in horror at the battle going on above him. Enderbrine, who was now a gigantic black tentacle monster, was fighting Herobrine, who had turned himself into a huge stone giant with glowing white eyes.

When Enderbrine had first monstermaxed, Wretch had been knocked out by one of the black tentacles that had sprouted from the monster's mouth. When he'd awoken, half the mountain had been destroyed, and Herobrine and Enderbrine had been in the middle of their battle.

Wham! Suddenly one of Enderbrine's black tentacles slapped Herobrine in the face, sending him tumbling down the mountain. Wretch watched from afar as the giant stone Herobrine tumbled down, down, down, destroying everything in its path. Finally, Herobrine managed to get to his feet once more and charged up the mountain towards his son. Enderbrine shot out more tentacles towards Herobrine, but this time Herobrine grabbed two of them, yanking them so hard that they broke. But Enderbrine seemed to have no limit to how many tentacles he could regrow, and more tentacles wrapped around Herobrine. Herobrine struggled, but the tentacles were too tight, and he couldn't break free.

That monster is going to kill Lord Herobrine, thought Wretch. If Herobrine was slain, Wretch didn't know if anyone else would be able to stop Enderbrine, and, more importantly, Herobrine's plan to destroy the world would never come to fruition—and that was not something Wretch could allow.

Ever since Wretch had learned of Herobrine's true plans, he'd been even more committed to the cause than before. The idea of destroying the world—of destroying all the people who had wronged him—was very appealing to Wretch. The world had treated him badly his entire life, and he wanted to get some revenge. Destroying the world would put an end to all the horribleness, all the suffering. Like Wretch himself, the world was a wretched and evil place that deserved to be obliterated.

Wham! Wham! Wham! Enderbrine smashed the giant stone Herobrine with his tentacles again and again. The stone Herobrine fell over, slamming into the mountain. As the mountain shattered, an avalanche of stone blocks and lava cascaded down the slope towards Wretch. He dived out of the way and just avoided getting flattened by the falling blocks.

Cling, cling!

Something metal landed next to Wretch. He looked over and saw that it was a trident: a familiar-looking silver trident.

The Trident of Hexaros, thought Wretch. It was Isabella's trident; the one that she claimed could remove powers.

Wretch picked up the trident. It felt lighter than he thought it would.

KA-WHAM!!!

Wretch looked up and saw Enderbrine deliver another ferocious blow to the giant stone Herobrine. Enderbrine's tentacle went right through the middle of the stone Herobrine's waist, and the stone Herobrine shattered into pieces. Even though he was far away, Wretch could see the tiny figure of Herobrine falling towards the ground in a shower of stone blocks.

"HUUUUUURRRGGGGH!!!!!" Enderbrine roared triumphantly. The colossal black tentacle monster had won the battle.

I have to save Lord Herobrine, thought Wretch. He picked up the trident and began clambering up the mountain, avoiding the falling blocks and the rivers of lava. Half of the mountain had been destroyed, and the half that remained was a ruin, so the going was tough.

Wretch had to clamber around pits that led down into the bowels of the earth and avoid lakes of lava that had overflowed their banks and were flowing down the mountain.

When I save Lord Herobrine, he will respect me above everyone else, thought Wretch. *He will know that I'm his only faithful servant: not his mad son, not those treacherous witches, me. Only me.*

Finally, Wretch reached the ruined plain that was now the top of the mountain. Enderbrine, the colossal black tentacle monster, was looking down triumphantly at his father. Herobrine was lying on the stone ground, looking up at his son.

One of Enderbrine's black tentacles reached down to try and grab Herobrine, but Herobrine held out his hand and blasted the tentacle with electricity. Enderbrine barely seemed to feel it, however, and wrapped his tentacle around Herobrine, until just Herobrine's face was showing out of the top.

"HURR, HURR HUUUUUUURR!" bellowed Enderbrine, his laughter echoing across the mountains. The one-eyed monster opened his mouth wide, preparing to eat his father.

Wretch ran forward towards Enderbrine, pumping his legs as fast as they would go.

I will save you, Lord Herobrine! he thought. *I will*

save you!

Wretch plunged the trident into one of Enderbrine's colossal black tentacles. For a moment, it looked like nothing would happen, but then the trident began to glow black, and Enderbrine began to scream.

As Enderbrine flailed in pain, he dropped his father, and Herobrine landed on the ground. The tentacle that Wretch had pushed the trident into lifted into the air, but Wretch didn't let go. The tentacle flailed up and down, but the trident stayed stuck inside it, and Wretch kept holding on.

"ARRRRAAAAAAAAGGGHHHHHH!!!!!!" Enderbrine roared.

Finally, Enderbrine collapsed, his tentacles resting on the ground. Suddenly, all of his tentacles began shrinking. The tentacle that the Trident of Hexaros had pierced was sucked away, back with all the other tentacles, all of them getting smaller and smaller as they were sucked back into Enderbrine's body. Finally, all the tentacles were gone, and Enderbrine was back in his normal form. He staggered on his feet for a few seconds then collapsed forward onto the stone ground.

Wretch ran over to Herobrine and helped him to his feet.

"Are you all right, My Lord?" Wretch asked.

Herobrine said nothing. He looked more furious than

Wretch had ever seen him.

Without a word, Herobrine marched over to his son, Wretch following behind him.

When they reached Enderbrine, the half-Herobrine half-enderman creature looked up at them from the ground with confusion in his eyes.

"Where... Where am I?" said Enderbrine, his voice sounding just like Herobrine's. "What's going on? I think I was having a nightmare... I can remember... I can remember doing such horrible things... Who am I? What happened to me?"

Herobrine said nothing; he just reached down and touched Enderbrine on the forehead. For a second, nothing happened, and then Enderbrine began to dissolve, turning into ash and floating away on the breeze.

"No..." gasped Enderbrine. "No, what's happening to me? What's—"

And then he was gone. Enderbrine was dead.

"What now, My Lord?" Wretch asked.

"Now I find Dave and end this once and for all," said Herobrine.

Herobrine knelt down and touched the ground, closing his eyes.

"He's still on this mountain," said Herobrine, "I can feel him..."

Herobrine opened his eyes and stood up. Then he flew

up, hovering into the air, then flew off down the side of the mountain.

Wretch was left all alone. He looked at the spot where Enderbrine had been, but now there was nothing left apart from a few flakes of ash.

Wretch looked at the trident in his hands, which was still glowing with black energy.

This must be all of Enderbrine's power, thought Wretch. He wondered what he should do with it. Was there a way he could dispose of the power? Should he drop the trident in lava?

And then Wretch realized what he needed to do. He had all this power here, in his hands, and there was no way he was going to waste it.

I will become your greatest servant, Lord Herobrine, Wretch thought. *I will be the most powerful servant you ever had! I will make you proud!*

And then Wretch plunged the trident into his chest. Instantly, he could feel Enderbrine's power flowing into him. For a moment, it hurt, and then it felt amazing. His whole body was tingling, filled with more power than he had ever known.

He collapsed to the floor, his body shuddering and shaking as the power flowed through him.

"HURR, HURR!" he laughed. "HEE, HEE, HOO!"

His mind was filled with terrible thoughts: he wanted

to kill, he wanted to eat, he wanted to destroy.

No, thought Wretch, *I need to control this! I don't want to end up like Enderbrine! I need to control this!*

Wretch could feel the madness infecting his brain. He couldn't stop laughing, and when he looked down, something that looked like black treacle was spreading across his hands.

Control this! Wretch told himself. *You can control this!*

CHAPTER SEVEN

The Cave

As they reached the bottom of the mountain, Dave and Jean-Cowphio led Spidroth and her siblings into a nearby cave. Spidroth, Vioroth, Slimoth and Necroth were all still exhausted from having their power removed. Dave had his arm around Spidroth to support her, Jean-Cowphio had his arm around Vioroth, and Necroth and Slimoth had their arms around each other, to keep themselves from falling.

They walked further into the cave, Dave placing torches as they went. A couple of zombies and one creeper tried to attack them, but Dave fought them off with the Shadow Blade. Finally, they reached a small cavern with enough room for them all to rest. Dave placed a few torches down to make sure no monsters disturbed them, and then he built four beds for Spidroth and her siblings. As soon as Spidroth, Vioroth, Slimoth and Necroth's heads hit their pillows, they went straight to sleep.

"Yo, you reckon we'll be safe down here?" Jean-

Cowphio asked Dave.

"I think so," said Dave. "I hope Carl and the others found somewhere safe as well. We need to hide until Herobrine and that monstrous son of his are long gone."

Jean-Cowphio took off his golden helmet and sat down next to Vioroth's bed.

"Man, I love Vee, but she's got one crazy family," said Jean-Cowphio, wiping the sweat from his brow.

"All of Herobrine's children have been through a lot," said Dave.

"Yeah, he's not gonna win any prizes for being a great dad," said Jean-Cowphio.

I ought to make some beds for me and Jean-Cowphio, Dave thought. It would probably be best if they all just slept until this was over.

Dave placed down a crafting table and was just about to build two more beds when *KRA-THOOOOSH!!!!!!!* Something blasted down through the ceiling.

"Oh no," said Jean-Cowphio, the color draining from his fur. "We're in trouble now!"

Herobrine stood in the middle of the cavern, surrounded by rubble.

"Hello, Dave," he said. "I found you."

Spidroth and her siblings began to wake up in their beds.

"Dad?" said Slimoth, looking sleepily at Herobrine.

"Oh man, am I having a nightmare?"

"No," said Herobrine, "but you will be soon. I will deal with the four of you in a minute, my children. Once Dave gives me the information that I need."

I need to get the Shadow Blade out, thought Dave. He had put it back in his rucksack.

"Father..." said Spidroth sleepily, "at last we meet again! At last, I can have my vengeance and..."

And then Spidroth fell back to sleep. Vioroth, Slimoth and Necroth had all gone back to sleep as well.

"Perhaps I'll banish all four of my children beneath the bedrock this time," Herobrine grinned, looking at Dave and Jean-Cowphio. "Then they can have all eternity to think about how they wronged me."

"Man, you are one messed up guy," said Jean-Cowphio. "I thought my mum was mean, but you're like a whole different flavor of mean."

"Stop your babbling," snapped Herobrine. "Now, Dave, our dance ends here. I will take the information I need from you now."

"The only thing you're gonna be taking is a kick!" said a voice. "A Kick in the butt!"

Dave looked over and saw Alex, Carl, Sensei Coach, Cluck Lee, his parents, the Ninja Squad and a massive army of amber chickens. Alex was the one who had spoken, and she stood at the front of everyone, holding a weird device that Dave had never seen before. The device was a large purple tube that Alex had resting on her shoulder. It seemed to be some sort of weapon, and she was aiming it right at Herobrine.

"Eat bedrock!" yelled Alex, and *BLAM, BLAM, BLAM,* she fired the weapon at Herobrine, covering him in thick grey-black liquid.

That's liquid bedrock, Dave realized.

"Take that, Loserbrine!" said Alex. "This is the *Bedrock Blaster*, created by a good friend of mine, Professor Quigley. In a few seconds, that bedrock is going to harden, and you're gonna be stuck like that forever!"

Just as Alex had said it would, the gloopy liquid bedrock began to harden, and Herobrine was stuck in position, like a statue.

"You did it, dear girl!" said Porkins happily. "That cad is defeated at last!"

There was a flash of white light, and suddenly Herobrine appeared in front of them, free from the bedrock.

"Did you really think that weapon would work on me?" Herobrine snarled, yanking it away from Alex and snapping in two. "I can teleport."

"Well, teleport away from this!" said Alex, charging towards Herobrine with her two diamond swords. The whole Ninja Squad joined her, charging at Herobrine as well, and Porkins began firing arrows at him.

Herobrine just stood there as the Ninja Squad whacked him with their swords, and Porkins hit him with arrows. None of the weapons did any damage at all.

While this was going on, Dave rummaged in his bag and pulled out the Shadow Blade.

This is my chance, he thought.

"ENOUGH!" roared Herobrine, holding out his hands and blasting Alex and the Ninja Squad with electricity. Alex went flying backward into Porkins and Jean-Cowphio, all three of them smashing against the wall. Carl charged at Herobrine, but Herobrine fired another bolt of electricity at him, sending the creeper flying back in his golem suit, skidding across the floor of the cavern.

Then Cluck Lee ran towards Herobrine. Herobrine fired a blast of electricity at him, but the chicken jumped out of the way, then booted Herobrine under the chin. It was a good kick, but Herobrine's chin was as hard as bedrock, and there was a nasty *CRUNCH* as Cluck Lee's leg broke.

"BWAAAAARK!!!" screeched Cluck Lee. Sensei Coach ran over and picked up his chicken.

Steve was the next one to run at Herobrine, clutching an iron sword in his hand. Herobrine turned and lazily blasted Steve with electricity, sending him flying as well.

Herobrine chuckled.

"Steve, I didn't expect you to be here, but I'm disappointed," said Herobrine. "I thought you'd be a more formidable opponent, judging by the stories I've heard about you, but I guess not."

Alex, Porkins, Carl, Steve, Jean-Cowphio and the Ninja Squad were all on the ground, still hurting from being hit by the electricity, and Spidroth and her siblings were still asleep in their beds. Dave was the only fighter left standing, and Herobrine turned to face him. Before Dave could react, Herobrine ran forward, moving so fast that he was a blur, and then placed his hand on Dave's forehead.

Dave gasped. He could feel Herobrine rummaging around inside his brain, sieving through his thoughts. He wanted to scream, but when he opened his mouth, nothing came out.

Finally, Herobrine took his hand away, and Dave fell to the floor.

"So, that's it," said Herobrine, smiling. "I can't believe it... After all these years... All I needed to do was combine blaze powder and ender pearls to make one of these *eye of ender* things. So simple..."

I can't let Herobrine escape, thought Dave, pushing himself to his feet. There was something in the End that Herobrine needed to destroy the world, and now that he knew the secret to ender eyes, he would be able to get there. He had to be stopped.

"Right," said Herobrine, "now I have what I need, I think I'll kill you all one by—"

Herobrine stopped talking as he noticed the Shadow Blade in Dave's hand.

"What is this, Dave?" Herobrine asked, a slight smile on his lips. "Is this some sort of magical weapon? Is it a weapon that you think will defeat me?"

"Maybe," said Dave, holding the Shadow Blade out in front of him.

"Even if that blade of yours does work against me," said Herobrine, "do you really think you'd even be able to hit me?"

Herobrine pulled out his own blade: the Ancient's obsidian sword with the quartz hilt.

"I'll tell you what," said Herobrine, "let's swordfight. Let's see if you can even land a hit on me."

Herobrine was playing with him like an ocelot playing with its food, Dave knew. Herobrine knew as well as he did that there was no chance that Dave would be able to beat him in a swordfight. If Herobrine was anywhere near as good at sword fighting as Spidroth was, Dave would get POOFed in less than a second, but what choice did he have?

Dave thought back to his sword training with Spidroth. All he needed was one lucky hit; one lucky strike.

I can do this, Dave thought to himself. *I can do this...*

"Time to die, Dave!" said Herobrine, and then he started to run towards him.

Dave ran towards Herobrine, clutching the Shadow Blade, both of them rushing to meet each other.

I can do this, I can do this, I can do this, thought Dave.

And then he realized something: he *couldn't* do this. Shadow Blade or no Shadow Blade, there was no way he could beat Herobrine in the sword fight. In less than a second, Herobrine's obsidian sword would slice right through him, and he would be POOFed.

And then Dave realized what he had to do. He stopped running, reached into his pocket and pulled out the Dimensional Portal Device.

Herobrine was running straight for him, pulling back the obsidian blade and getting ready to strike Dave down. Herobrine jumped up, flying through the air straight towards Dave, and Dave pressed the button on the Dimensional Portal Device.

FSSHAM!

The rectangular blue portal appeared in midair in front of Dave. Dave could see through the portal slightly, and for a second, he saw the fear in Herobrine's eyes, and then Herobrine flew straight into the portal, disappearing from sight. Dave threw the Dimensional Portal Device onto the ground and then stabbed it with the Shadow Blade

FKKKKSHHHHAMMM!!!!!!!!

The Dimensional Portal Device exploded, and, at the same moment, the blue portal vanished. Everyone looked on in shock. There was no sign of Herobrine.

"What happened to Herobrine?" Alex asked, getting to her feet.

"He's gone," said Dave, breathing a sigh of relief. "He's trapped in the Mirror Universe."

CHAPTER EIGHT

Wretch Reborn

The sun was starting to go down, and Wretch was starting to lose his grasp on his sanity.

His brain felt like it was full of silverfish, and it took all his willpower not to just start laughing.

It's these powers, thought Wretch. *They drove Enderbrine crazy, but I'm not going to let them drive me crazy too. I can control them. I know I can!*

Wretch fell to the ground, clutching his head.

Control it! he told himself. *Control it!*

Wretch concentrated as hard as he could, trying to keep his thoughts in check. He closed his eyes, taking long, deep breaths.

Then he heard the voices. Strange, croaky voices, unlike anything he'd ever heard before.

"What's up," said one of the voices.

"Hey," said another.

"Look for the eye," said a third.

Wretch opened his eyes and saw that he was

surrounded by endermen. As soon as the endermen saw him watching them, they opened their mouths, screamed and charged towards him.

"No!" yelled Wretch. "Leave me alone!"

And, to Wretch's surprise, the endermen stopped.

The endermen did as I commanded, thought Wretch. He thought back to something that the witches had said: that Enderbrine had initially been designed to control endermen. From the stories that Wretch had heard, all of Herobrine's children could control different types of mobs, and Enderbrine had been built to control endermen. Of course, in the end, Enderbrine had proved to be too insane to do anything apart from kill and eat things, but maybe that power to control endermen had been inside him all along, and now it was inside Wretch.

"Dance," Wretch said to the endermen. "I command you to dance."

The endermen began to dance. Their movements were weird and strange, but it was definitely some kind of dance.

I can command endermen, thought Wretch happily. *I will be able to build Lord Herobrine an army full of endermen soldiers.*

Wretch felt a drop of water land on his cheek, then the heavens opened and it started to rain. The endermen all began to scream and panic, and then teleported away, leaving Wretch on his own once more. He lay on his back, enjoying the cool feeling of the rain on his skin.

"Is that Wretch?" he heard a voice say.

Wretch sat up and saw a group of witches in blue robes walking towards him. They were Herobrine's witches.

"Ugh, what's happened to your skin?" said the witch called Esrelda, looking with disgust at Wretch. "And your eyes..."

"Where is Lord Herobrine?" Wretch asked the witches. "Did he get what he needed from Dave?"

"Lord Herobrine has been defeated," said Esrelda. "We came across Dave the villager and his friends as we were searching for Herobrine. We sneaked up and heard them talking: apparently Dave used some magical device to trap Lord Herobrine in an alternate universe."

"Then we have to save him," said Wretch. "We have to get Lord Herobrine back!"

Another one of the witches laughed.

"No chance," she said. "My days of serving Lord Herobrine are over."

"Mine too," said another witch. "He treats us like slaves, he doesn't respect our opinions and he let his son eat us."

"I used to respect Lord Herobrine, but ever since he was imprisoned in New Diamond City, he's changed for the worse," said Esrelda. "This whole plan to lure Dave up to the top of that mountain was foolish from the start. If Lord Herobrine had listened to us, then he wouldn't be in this mess."

"I say, let him rot in that alternative universe," said another witch. "He deserves it."

The other witches muttered in agreement.

"I'm sorry you feel that way," said Wretch, feeling the anger bubbling up inside him. How could these witches talk that way? Did they not see Lord Herobrine for the great man he was? Wretch wanted to punish them. He wanted to make them pay.

Suddenly Wretch felt something slithering at the back of his throat. He opened his mouth and a large white tentacle flopped out, landing on the ground. The witches screamed and began to run away, but it was too late. More white tentacles shot out of Wretch's mouth, wrapping around the witches.

The witches screamed and begged for mercy, but Wretch had no desire to show them any. He lifted the witches into the air with his white tentacle tongues. The witches struggled to break free, but the tentacles were wrapped too tightly around them.

"Wretch, don't do this!" shouted Esrelda. "What did we ever do to you?"

"Ever since I joined Lord Herobrine, you all treated

me like I was weak and worthless," said Wretch. "You all looked down at me because I wasn't as powerful as you, but now I'm far more powerful than you could ever imagine."

Wretch opened his jaws wide, far wider than he ever had before, and began sucking the tongues back into his mouth. The witches all screamed and screamed, and then they disappeared down his throat.

Wretch couldn't feel anything in his stomach. He'd just eaten six fully-grown witches, but he didn't even feel full.

"Hurr, hurr," he giggled. "Hurr, hurr, hurr, HURR!!!"

Wretch was seized by a fit of uncontrollable laughter. He raised his head to the sky, the rain splashing down on his face, and he laughed, and he laughed, and he laughed.

CHAPTER NINE

Pumpkin Pie

"Is he going to be okay, vet-san?" asked Sensei Coach.

"His leg will be healed within three weeks," said the vet, "but I advise that he doesn't do any kung-fu for at least six months."

"What about judo?" asked Sensei Coach.

"No martial arts of any kind."

The vet's assistant came out, pushing Cluck Lee along in a tiny wheelchair. The chicken's leg was in a cast.

"Bwark!" said Cluck Lee.

"Oh, Cluck Lee," said Sensei Coach, kneeling down next to the chicken, "you fought so bravely! I'll make sure you have all the wheat seeds you can eat."

"Bwark!" said Cluck Lee.

Dave, Carl, Porkins, Steve, Jean-Cowphio, Spidroth, Vioroth, Slimoth, Necroth, Sensei Coach and around fifty amber chickens were all gathered outside the front of the veterinary surgery in Spectrite City.

"Dave-san, I'm going to take Cluck Lee back home,"

said Sensei Coach.

"Of course," said Dave. "That chicken of yours is a good fighter."

Spidroth knelt down next to Cluck Lee's wheelchair.

"You fought like a true warrior," she said to the chicken. "Thank you for helping us."

"Bwark!" said Cluck Lee.

Sensei Coach grabbed Cluck Lee's wheelchair and wheeled him away down the street, followed by all the chickens.

"And thanks to all of you too," Dave said to the others. "Without all of us working together, we would never have been able to defeat Herobrine."

"Do you think that idiot is really gone for good?" Carl asked.

"I can't see how he'd get back," said Dave. "With the Dimensional Portal Device destroyed, he's got no way of returning to our universe."

"I can't believe I slept through the battle with our father," said Necroth. "It's very embarrassing."

"Dude, I'm glad I slept through it," said Slimoth.

"Dave, dear, I don't think I will ever be able to thank you enough for what you've done," said Vioroth. "For years, our father plagued our lives, but now we're finally free of him."

"You did well, Dave," said Spidroth, smiling at Dave.

Dave felt his cheeks start to glow.

*

No one in Spectrite City knew who Herobrine was, so there was no parade or celebration to mark that he had been defeated. Instead, Dave and the others went out for a big meal at one of Spectrite City's fanciest restaurants. Necroth picked up the bill.

Necroth also paid for them to get rooms at a fancy hotel near the city center. From his bedroom window, Dave could see the half-built statues of Steve and Cluck Lee in the city square, both of them surrounded by scaffolding.

They both deserve those statues, Dave thought. It felt weird to be mourning someone who was still alive, but Dave found himself thinking about the old version of Steve: the one who used to say *bro* all the time. Dave always used to find it so annoying, but he would have loved to have heard the old Steve say it one last time.

Necroth had paid for them all to have individual rooms, so, for once, Dave lay in bed with only his own thoughts for company.

I can't believe Herobrine is gone for good, Dave thought to himself. It didn't seem real. It seemed too good to be true.

Dave was just glad that Herobrine wouldn't be able to hurt anyone ever again. He'd ruined so many lives: his children, the pigmen, Robo-Steve and countless others.

For once, Dave slept peacefully. He had no weird dreams about endermen or dragons or eggs. In fact, he didn't dream at all. When he woke the next morning, he felt calm and refreshed for the first time in a long time.

*

Spidroth was happier than she had ever been in her life. She'd spent the last three days hanging out in Spectrite City with her siblings, going for walks, seeing the sites and talking. It was like the four of them had never been apart. In fact, they were getting on better than they ever had before. Their whole lives, the shadow of Herobrine had hung over everything they'd done, but now Spidroth, Vioroth, Slimoth and Necroth were free. They had no-one to fear and could do what they wanted. Yes, they'd lost their powers, but none of them really cared. Herobrine was gone: and that was the most important thing.

As the sun went down on the third day, Spidroth, Vioroth, Slimoth and Necroth sat on a bench in Spectrite City Park, eating pumpkin pies that they'd bought from a local vendor.

"Dude, this pumpkin pie is good, but not as good as

yours, Vioroth," said Slimoth, wiping the crumbs from his mouth.

"Thank you, brother," smiled Vioroth. "You know, if you all come back to Cow Village with me, you can have pumpkin pie every day."

"You would want us to come back with you?" asked Necroth.

"Of course!" said Vioroth. "I haven't seen you all for far too many years. We should be together."

"Sounds good to me," said Slimoth, stuffing another piece of pumpkin pie into his mouth. "Living as a lake was getting a bit boring anyway."

"I would also like to take you up on that offer, sister," said Necroth. "I can pay some builders to move my mansion to Cow Village block by block."

"Dude, won't that be a bit expensive?" said Slimoth.

"Yes, I imagine it will be," said Necroth. "But unlike you, brother, I have made wise investments over the years. I have invested in the Spectrite City stock-market and have put my emeralds in several high-profile funds that—"

"Okay, okay," said Slimoth, "we get it. You're a nerd."

"It is not nerdy to invest your money wisely!" said Necroth, his cheeks glowing pink.

"Nah, man, it is," said Slimoth. "If I ever get any emeralds, I always spend them straight away. That's why my life is so fun."

"My life is fun too!" said Necroth. "Just because I'm not an irresponsible little—"

"That's enough, you two," laughed Vioroth. "What about you, sister? Will you join us? Your friends Dave and Carl could come live with us too."

Spidroth sighed. She wanted to say yes, to join her siblings in Cow Village, but she knew that she couldn't.

"I'm sorry," she said. "Maybe one day, but I want to continue the quest I'm on. I want to go to the End with Dave. I mean, with Dave and Carl," she added quickly.

"Dude, what's the deal with you and that Dave guy anyway?" asked Slimoth. "Is he your boyfriend?"

"We're just friends," said Spidroth quickly.

"Oh man, you liiiiiike him," teased Slimoth.

"That's enough, brother," said Necroth. "Leave Spidroth alone."

"Okay, okay," said Slimoth, rolling his eyes. "I was just messing about."

"Yes, I know," said Necroth. "It seems that messing about is all that you ever do."

Spidroth laughed. Seeing her brothers arguing like this, just like in the old days, made her heart feel all nice and fuzzy.

"You'll come and visit us once you've defeated the ender dragon, though, won't you? said Vioroth.

"Of course," said Spidroth, giving her sister a smile.

"Just you try and stop me."

"I hate to change the subject, but there's something that's been preying on my mind," said Necroth. "Do you think that villager with the brown hair was telling the truth —about Enderbrine being our brother?"

"I wouldn't put it past dad to make some crazy monster like that," said Slimoth. "I just wish we could have saved the dude. I mean, he was pretty crazy and evil, but we all used to be pretty crazy and evil too. We did some bad things in Dad's name, back in the day. Yeah, we turned against Dad in the end, but we followed his orders for a long time."

"You're right," said Spidroth, "we can't erase all the bad things we did for father. They happened, and it's something we'll all have to live with. All we can do now is try to make amends for what we've done and make this world a better place in any way we can."

"Well said, sister," said Necroth.

"Yeah, well said, sis," said Slimoth. "Now, are you going to finish that slice of pumpkin pie?"

CHAPTER TEN

Farewell to Spectrite City

Dave found Alex in the park, in the middle of training the Ninja Squad.

"And block and parry and parry and block!" said Alex, waving her wooden sword about. The Ninja Squad all followed her motions with their own wooden swords.

"Why do we have to do sword training?" asked Lila. "Sasha and I are archers."

"To truly be a kick-butt warrior, you have to be good with all weapons," said Alex. "We'll all be doing some archery this afternoon."

"Hey, Alex," said Dave, walking over to her. "How's it going?"

Oh, hey, Dave!" said Alex. "All right, you lot," she said to the Ninja Squad, "practice on your own for a bit."

Dave noticed that the Ninja Squad had a new member: Steve was there, wearing black and practicing with a wooden sword along with the rest of them.

"What's Steve doing?" Dave whispered to Alex.

"Oh, he wanted to join the squad," said Alex. "Apparently, he's been reading a load of *Seth the Elf* comics, and now he wants to be a ninja."

"Um, good for him, I guess," said Dave. Ever since Steve had re-spawned, he'd seemed at a bit of a loss about what to do. Maybe hanging out with the Ninja Squad was just what he needed, Dave thought.

"So," said Dave, as he and Alex took a walk through the park, "I just wanted to say thank you again. You know, for coming all this way to save me and the others."

"Well, in the end, I didn't do much saving," sighed Alex. "That Bedrock Blaster that Professor Quigley made was pretty cool, but it didn't really do anything against Herobrine."

"Alex," said Dave, "there's something I need to tell you. This is going to sound a bit strange, but I met Robo-Steve. After he died."

"You're right," said Alex, "that does sound a bit strange."

"There's this place called the Phantom Realm," said Dave. "It's hard to explain, but it's a place that people go to when they die. Carl, Spidroth and I went down there, and we met Robo-Steve. That's how I knew he had died. He told me to tell you that he was very proud of you."

Alex began to cry.

"That's... Thanks, Dave," she said, wiping her eyes.

Then she leaned forward and gave Dave a big hug. Dave patted her on the back.

"Robo Steve was a true hero," said Dave. "Even death couldn't stop him from being a hero. He helped me, Carl and Spidroth to escape the Phantom Realm. Without his help, we would still be stuck down there."

"Dave, I've been thinking," said Alex, "would it be all right if I join you on your quest again? The Ninja Squad will be fine without me, and I don't really fancy returning to New Diamond City. If I go back there, I'll just be thinking about Robo Steve all the time."

"Of course you can come with us," said Dave. "We'd love to have you back."

"Are you sure your girlfriend won't mind?" Alex asked. "You know, the pretty one with the red skin."

"I... Spidroth isn't my girlfriend," said Dave, feeling his cheeks glowing red.

"Really?" said Alex. "Sorry, Dave, I just thought she was. You know, because you two are always looking at each other all the time."

"Er, lovely weather we're having today," said Dave, hastily trying to change the subject.

Dave heard the sound of heavy footsteps and turned around to see Carl and Porkins walking towards them. Carl was in his golem suit.

"All right, bozos," said Carl. "How's it going?"

"Alex is going to join us on the quest," said Dave.

"Oh, what spiffing news!" said Porkins.

"Good to have you back, Alex," said Carl. "If we had Robo-Steve here, we'd have all the original team back together."

Carl fell silent, realizing what he'd said. For a moment, the four of them didn't know what to say.

"We will continue our quest to honor Robo-Steve, said Porkins. "It's what the dear chap would have wanted."

"For Robo-Steve," Carl agreed.

"For Robo-Steve," said Dave.

Alex wiped the tears from her eyes.

"For Robo-Steve," she said. "Now come on, let's go and get some delicious cake to cheer us up."

*

After four days in Spectrite City, Dave finally found the chance to talk to Spidroth, while the two of them were walking home from a cake-eating competition. Dave hadn't been participating in the competition himself, but Alex, Steve and Slimoth had been. Alex had won the competition easily, winning the prize of 100 emeralds. Everyone had been there: Dave, Carl, Porkins, Alex, Steve, Dave's parents, Jean-Cowphio, the Ninja Squad and Spidroth and her three siblings.

After the competition was over, they'd all left together, walking back through the rainbow streets in the moonlight. Somehow, Dave and Spidroth had both taken a wrong turn and got separated from the others. It was the first time that they had been alone together in a very long while, and Dave found it difficult to know what to say.

"Um, I'm glad you're not a chicken anymore," Dave said.

"Yes, me too," said Spidroth.

Why is this so hard? thought Dave. *Just tell her how you feel.*

"Dave," said Spidroth, "about that kiss... I... I think that was a mistake. I haven't had many friends in my life. In fact, apart from my brothers and sister, I haven't really had any friends at all. I don't want anything to ruin the friendship that you and I have. I... I hope you understand."

Dave wanted to tell Spidroth how he really felt. He wanted to ask her to be his girlfriend, but instead he said...

"I understand."

Then, to Dave's surprise, Spidroth hugged him.

"Out of all the fools I know," said Spidroth, "you're my favorite."

Dave said nothing; he just held Spidroth in his arms.

"One thing, though," said Spidroth, "if you tell the creeper that I hugged you, I'll throw you off a cliff."

"Okay," laughed Dave, "I promise not to tell him."

"You'd better not," said Spidroth.

Dave was sad that Spidroth didn't want to be his girlfriend, but he understood. He didn't want to lose her friendship either. Dave and Spidroth had been through a lot, from meeting underneath the bedrock when she was still a giant spider-monster, to meeting her again as an angry potato, to having her tag along with him and Carl when she was a chicken, to her getting her body back, to her losing her body again, to her getting her body back once more.

"Come on," said Dave, "let's go and catch up with the others."

*

The next day, Steve and the Ninja Squad said their goodbyes to the others outside of the inn.

"We ought to be getting back to our continent," Alice told Dave. "There was some trouble brewing when we left, with quite a few illager raids going down."

"I know all about those illager blighters," said Porkins bitterly. "An illager named Pumpkin Head wiped out my village."

"I'm sorry to hear that," said Ash. "We captured Pumpkin Head before Herobrine stole our powers, so he won't be able to hurt anyone anymore."

"I'm jolly glad to hear that," smiled Porkins. "If any more of those illager rotters try anything, I hope you show them what's what."

"Not all illagers are bad," said Dave, thinking about Chonky and Ivy and the rest of the illagers on their island.

"Pah," said Porkins. "No offense, Dave old bean, but I'll believe that when I see it."

Dave couldn't blame Porkins for being prejudiced against illagers. An illager gang had wiped out all of his people. If the same thing had happened to Dave, he probably wouldn't be able to trust illagers either.

"I hope you don't mind me going off with the ninjas," Steve said to Dave. "Your quest to find the Dragon sounds cool and all, but being a ninja sounds even cooler."

"Of course I don't mind," smiled Dave. In reality, if he was being honest, Dave was actually quite happy that Steve had given up the quest to slay the ender dragon. Ever since Dave had begun his journey, all that time ago, he'd been racing to get to the End before Steve, and now he no longer had to worry about him. Steve was a fantastic warrior, and Dave knew that he would make a great ninja. Their continent would be safe with the Ninja Squad there to guard it.

Dave's parents were going back with the Ninja Squad as well. Dave's mum and dad came over and both gave him a big hug.

"Look after yourself, son," said Dave's dad.

"Are you sure you won't come home with us?" asked Dave's mum. "I know everyone would love to see you again."

"Dave has an adventure to go on," said Dave's dad, putting a hand on his son's shoulder. "He'll be fine."

"Thanks, Dad," smiled Dave. "As soon as I've completed my quest, I'll come straight back and see you guys."

"We'll leave a space above the fireplace to mount that dragon's head," said Dave's dad, with a smile.

Dave thanked his mum and dad, but his dad's comment about the dragon's head stuck in his mind. There was something that he had been thinking about a lot, and the thought of the dragon's head brought it all up again.

When Steve, the Ninja Squad and Dave's parents had all set off, Dave asked Carl, Porkins, Alex and Spidroth to join him in the small garden at the back of the inn.

"I've been thinking," said Dave, "I don't want to kill the ender dragon."

"What do you mean?" said Carl. "You want to give up the quest?"

"No," said Dave. "I still want to find the end portal, and I still want to reach the End, but why do we need to kill the dragon?"

"Because it's a dragon," shrugged Carl. "Heroes kill

dragons."

"But we've no idea if this dragon is good or bad," said Dave. "We can't just go to its home and kill it—what right do we have to do that?"

"Aw man," said Carl, "I guess you're right."

"I think that's a jolly good decision, Dave," said Porkins. "I've seen enough death and destruction recently to last me a lifetime."

"I agree," said Spidroth.

"Your dad is going to be disappointed when you don't bring that dragon head back to put above his fireplace," Carl said Dave.

"He'll get over it," laughed Dave.

That afternoon, it was Vioroth, Slimoth and Necroth's turn to leave.

"Goodbye, sister," Vioroth said, giving Spidroth a big hug. "Dave, you make sure that you look after her. She's not as strong as she makes out."

"Please, sister," said Spidroth, "stop embarrassing me."

"Come here, sis!" said Slimoth, hugging Spidroth and lifting her into the air. "Make sure you come and see us when you get back!"

"Yes, my mansion should be rebuilt in Cow Village by the time you return," said Necroth. "I will make sure that you are given the master bedroom."

"Hey, why can't I sleep in the master bedroom?" said Slimoth.

"Because you are an unwashed oaf," said Necroth. "I wouldn't even let you sleep in the servants quarters."

"Yo, it's been emotional," said Jean-Cowphio, giving Dave, Carl and Spidroth all hugs. "When I write my awesome autobiography, this will get at least half a chapter."

Vioroth, Jean-Cowphio, Slimoth and Necroth all headed off. Necroth had bought them some horses in Spectrite City, and they all rode off across the snowy plains, towards the mountains. The mountain range around Spectrite City looked very different from when Dave and the others had first arrived: Half of Jeb's Peak had been completely demolished, and it was now one of the smallest mountains in the range, no longer towering above the others.

*

After staying another night at the inn, Dave, Carl, Spidroth, Alex and Porkins left Spectrite City. Dave led them all back to the abandoned castle— the one that they'd been staying in when they'd first seen Herobrine's message in the sky.

"Why are we back in this dump?" Carl asked.

"Shouldn't you be throwing an eye of ender into the sky or something?"

"I will," said Dave, but there's something I need to do first."

Dave dug a hole in the middle of the courtyard, digging diagonally down. When he'd gone a few blocks beneath the ground, he placed down a wooden chest and opened it.

"What are you doing, old bean?" Porkins asked.

Dave took the Shadow Blade from his rucksack.

"Herobrine is probably gone for good," said Dave, "but I'm leaving this here in case he ever returns."

"Why don't you just bring it with you, you idiot?" asked Carl.

"I'm leaving it here in case something happens to me," said Dave. "This weapon may be the only thing that can defeat Herobrine. I'm leaving it here so that if Herobrine returns, one of us can reclaim it and use it to defeat him. If I brought it with me, I might lose it or drop in lava or something. The Shadow Blade is too valuable."

Dave placed the Shadow Blade in the wooden chest, and then went up and sealed the hole again, placing mossy cobblestone blocks above it so that it blended in with the rest of the courtyard.

"Dave, you have given up a powerful weapon," said Spidroth. "I hope you don't live to regret it."

"I'll be ok," said Dave. "I've got one netherite sword, and when that breaks I can always go back to the Nether and make another one."

"Well, what now?" Carl asked.

Dave reached into his bag and took out an eye of ender.

"Let's go on some more adventures," said Dave. He threw the ender eye up into the air. It hovered for a moment, then zoomed off towards the horizon, and Dave and his friends followed it.

*

"I'm hungry," moaned Carl.

Dave, Carl, Spidroth, Alex and Porkins had been walking through a desert biome for a week, and their food supplies were starting to get low.

"Wait," said Dave, squinting. "There's someone up ahead... I think it's a wandering trader."

"Maybe he has some food," said Carl excitedly.

The wandering trader wore the same blue, gold and red robes as the wandering traders did back on the villager continent, but he wasn't a villager, he was a cowman. He had a white llama following him.

"Hello there, fellow travelers," said the trader. "What can I do you for?"

"Enough chit chat," said Carl. "What grub do you have?"

The wandering trader went over to his llama and rummaged around in one of the pouches attached to the animal's back.

"Okay," he said, "let's see what we've got here... I've got some pumpkins, some carrots, a few fish—although I'm not sure how fresh they are—oh, and some weird vegetables I got from another trader. I can't remember what they're called."

The trader took a yellowy-brown vegetable from his bag and showed it to them.

"I've got loads of these things," he said. "I can let you have them for cheap if you want."

"Potatoes..." said Carl, his voice cracking with emotion. "Potatoes!"

Dave looked at the creeper and was amazed to see that Carl was crying: tears of joy running down his face.

"I think we'll take all of them," grinned Dave. "Give us all the potatoes you've got."

EPILOGUE

Chops put the finishing touches on another netherite golem, connecting the redstone circuit inside of it and turning it on. The golem stood up, its eyes glowing red.

"Good," she muttered to herself. "Good, good, good."

That was six golems so far. It wasn't much, but every empire had to start somewhere, she thought.

Chops reached for some more netherite ingots, but there were none left on the pile.

"No!" she snapped. What was she going to do? She could never reclaim her empire with only six golems.

"I'll use these golems to force the piglins to dig up more netherite for me," she muttered to herself. "Yes, yes, that's what I'll do."

Chops's castle had been destroyed, but she had built herself a small netherrack workshop next to the ruins. She had dug her old white coat and goggles out of the ruins as well and was wearing them as she worked on the golems. Thankfully, she had arms and legs again, thanks to the new gold-and-netherite body that Herobrine had built for her. Without that body, she would just have been a skull.

"Empress!" someone yelled from outside.

Chops scampered over to one of the windows, cautiously peering out of it. There was a villager outside, surrounded by an army of endermen. The villager was unlike any villager that chops had ever seen. His skin was as white as bone, the hair on the top of his head was jet black, and he had the pink eyes of an enderman. He wore black robes as well and was carrying an iron trident. Chops was sure that she hadn't met this villager before, but there was still something familiar about him.

Chops opened the door of the workshop and walked outside.

"What do you want?" she asked. "I've got an army of netherite golems in there," she added, motioning to the workshop. "If I give the word, they'll come out here and destroy you."

"I'm not here to fight you, Empress," said the villager, "I'm here because I want you to join me."

"Wait," said Chops, "I know you... You're that villager who was with Herobrine. What happened to your skin? And your eyes?"

"I want you to join me," repeated the villager, ignoring her question.

"And why would I do that?" asked Chops. "I have an

empire to rebuild here in the Nether. I don't have any time to be wasting with you and Herobrine and your foolish plans."

"I know that an empire isn't really what you want," said the villager. "You want the same thing as me: you want to destroy your enemies and burn the world for what it's done to you. I can offer you that. Join me, and we can destroy the world together—the overworld, the Nether, the End, all of it. We can wipe out every block, every mob, everything. How does that sound?"

"And how would we do that?" Chops asked, studying the villager's face to see if he was serious. "Where is Herobrine? Why did he send you instead of coming himself?"

"Herobrine has been imprisoned," said the villager. "But if you join me, the two of us can set him free."

"Herobrine turned my people into zombies!" snapped Chops. "Why would I want to free him?"

"They weren't your people, though, were they?" said the villager. "Your tribe left the Nether long before Herobrine cursed the pigmen. He's not the one to blame for your suffering: this cold and unfeeling universe is. If you trust me, we can help bring an end to this universe. We can destroy it all."

"Trust you?" said Chops. "Why should I trust you? I don't even know your name."

"I've had a few names," said the villager. "My parents called me Adam and Herobrine called me Wretch, but now I have a new name. One that I've chosen for myself. I decided to name myself in the manner of Herobrine's ungrateful children since I'm more of a son to him than his true sons ever were."

"Well, what shall I call you?" Chops demanded. "I haven't got all day."

"*Adaroth,*" said the villager, with a grin. "My name is *Adaroth.*"

*

Herobrine looked out at the endless expanse of white, feeling bitterly jealous.

A whole universe, gone, he thought. *How marvelous.*

This was everything that he had ever dreamed of: a dead universe with no life, no blocks, nothing at all. But this wasn't *his* universe; this was some alternate dimension. Herobrine had heard stories of alternate universes, tales of parallel worlds that could be reached through the Far Lands, but they had never interested him. All he cared about was destroying his *own* universe.

He looked around for a portal; for anything that could bring him back to his world. But he saw nothing.

When he'd first realized that he was trapped here,

Herobrine's instinct had been to rant and rage, but he had held his anger in check. Ever since he'd escaped his prison in New Diamond City, Herobrine had been letting his emotions get the better of him. That was what had led him to release Enderbrine; that was what had made him sword fight Dave, instead of just blasting him from afar with a bolt of lightning.

You must be calm and logical like you were in the past, Herobrine told himself. He knew the secret to finding end portals now, so all he had to do was get back to his old universe. Then he could reach the End, find the dragon egg and finish all this once and for all.

He was trapped in this dead universe for now, but that didn't mean he had to waste his time here. Herobrine raised his hands and created a swirling shadow in front of him. The shadow twisted and churned, Herobrine using his magic to mold its shape.

Finally, a shadow golem stood in front of him, this one much larger than the old ones he had made.

"One down," smiled Herobrine, looking up at the golem. "A whole army to go."

TO BE CONTINUED...

Made in the USA
Coppell, TX
11 March 2021